JORDAN AND MAX
SHOWTIME

SUZANNE SUTHERLAND

illustrated by
MICHELLE SIMPSON

ORCA BOOK PUBLISHERS

Printed in Canada and the United States in 2021 by Orca Book Publishers.
orcabook.com

Library and Archives Canada Cataloguing in Publication
Title: Jordan and Max, showtime / Suzanne Sutherland ; illustrated by Michelle Simpson.
Other titles: Showtime
Names: Sutherland, Suzanne, 1987- author. | Simpson, Michelle (Illustrator), illustrator.
Series: Orca echoes.
Description: Series statement: Orca echoes
Identifiers: Canadiana (print) 20210094796 | Canadiana (ebook) 20210094923 |
ISBN 9781459826953 (softcover) | ISBN 9781459826960 (PDF) |
ISBN 9781459826977 (EPUB)
Classification: LCC PS8637.U865 J67 2021 | DDC jc813/.6—dc23

Library of Congress Control Number: 2020951490

Summary: In this illustrated early chapter book, a young boy has trouble fitting in at his new
school until an unlikely friendship gives him the courage to show his true self to his classmates.

Orca Book Publishers is committed to reducing the consumption of
nonrenewable resources in the making of our books. We make every
effort to use materials that support a sustainable future.

Orca Book Publishers gratefully acknowledges the support for its publishing
programs provided by the following agencies: the Government of Canada,
the Canada Council for the Arts and the Province of British Columbia
through the BC Arts Council and the Book Publishing Tax Credit.

Cover and interior artwork by Michelle Simpson
Design by Dahlia Yuen
Edited by Liz Kemp
Author photo by Graham Christian

Printed and bound in Canada.

24 23 22 21 • 1 2 3 4

For Sheila Barry.

CHAPTER ONE

As he watched his grandmother's car pull out of the parking lot of his brand-new school, Jordan's many worries gathered together in his stomach and threw a wild party.

Jordan hadn't wanted a big scene when they arrived, and his grand-mother—who insisted that he call her Beverly, because that was her name—had promised that she wouldn't give her grandson a kiss, or call him Jordy, or do anything at all to embarrass him when she dropped him off for his first day. Since Beverly was already late for work, she'd only said a quick goodbye as her grandson got out of the car. But now Jordan was regretting not asking for a hug. Just a small one. For courage.

Jordan watched the other kids on the schoolyard as they buzzed together in clusters of friends, laughing and talking in what sounded like a whole different language. Their excitement only made him feel more lonely, like he was a visitor from a faraway planet. Like he was the only one of his kind.

True, he'd felt like an alien at his old school too, but at least there he knew what to expect. He knew the kids who thought his hair was funny because it hung almost to his chin, and the kids

who teased him about his belly, which stuck out in front of him and was the palest shade of white. He knew exactly what time to leave at the end of the day to avoid his worst critics in the schoolyard, and which teachers he could complain to about having a stomachache, the ones who would let him go down to the nurse's office until he felt better—or until it was time to go home, whichever came first.

This new school was an unknown world.

There was one kid, Jordan noticed, who hadn't clustered up with anyone else. He sat at the top of the playground slide, scribbling in a notebook and looking much too busy to care about anyone else. He had dark skin and a cloud of curly hair, a pair of mirrored sunglasses, and a flower-print button-up that opened to reveal a T-shirt with words Jordan could read from all the way across the yard—*NO THANKS.*

Just looking at those words sent the party in Jordan's stomach into a frenzy. It felt like a very bad sign.

At his old school, Jordan had tried his hardest to be invisible. True, it hadn't always worked, but as far as Jordan could tell, it was the only way to make it through the day without some kind of trouble. Would there be less trouble at his new school? He wasn't sure.

But there was no time to dwell on it. Just then the school's intercom sounded a long, low tone.

It was time for class.

CHAPTER TWO

As the students in Jordan's classroom took their seats, their teacher stood up and addressed the group.

"Welcome," she said. "My name is Ms. Davenport. I'm looking forward to getting to know each one of you this year. To start, why don't we go around the room and introduce ourselves?"

Each of Jordan's classmates sat up straight in their chairs as Ms. Davenport called on them one by one. As they spoke,

Jordan tried to remember their names, but as they went on, each kid began to blur into the next, and soon it was hard to remember any of their names at all.

When Jordan's turn came, he spoke in a small voice. "Hi," he said, "I'm Jordan."

"Hi, Jordan," said the class.

Then Jordan froze. Each of his classmates had introduced themselves by sharing an interesting fact or a funny story about their summer—but Jordan didn't feel like sharing. When he'd shared at his old school, it hadn't always turned out so well.

Still, he had to say something.

"I'm Jordan," he repeated, "and I live with my grandmother."

"Terrific," said Ms. Davenport. "Thank you, Jordan." Then she pointed to the next student.

Taking a deep breath, Jordan could still feel his worries whooping it up in his stomach, but he tried his best to ignore them. So far, he was still invisible. Maybe this new school *would* be different.

After the rest of his classmates had spoken, there was only one student left.

Jordan recognized him—the boy from the playground, with his shirt that said *NO THANKS*.

The boy stood up at his desk, and all around him Jordan heard whispers and giggles. Clearly the other students knew this boy well.

"Hello," he said, clutching a fist to his chest like a politician giving a rousing speech. "My name is Max, and I'm going to be a star."

A collective groaned rolled its way around the classroom. This obviously wasn't the first time Max had made this sort of pronouncement.

He continued. "I can sing, I can dance, and I can act. I'm a triple threat!" He dusted his knuckles against his shirt. "Plus I write all my own material, which makes me a *quadruple* threat."

Max pulled his sunglasses out of his pocket and began striking theatrical poses, mugging it up for an unseen camera.

"That's wonderful, Max," said Ms. Davenport. "You can take a seat now."

Around the room there were more giggles.

Jordan made a mental note that No Thanks Max attracted a lot of attention. If Jordan was going to be invisible at his new school, he'd need to keep his distance.

CHAPTER THREE

At home that night, Beverly made Jordan's favorite meal—corn fritters. She whisked together the batter and poured it into the sputtering frying pan, flipping the fritters onto their backs as they started to bubble. Pretty soon the whole house smelled buttery and delicious, and Jordan set the dining room table for two.

When they sat down with their piping-hot plates—the fritters stacked high on each, with an extra pat of butter on top—Beverly asked Jordan about his first day at school.

"Well…" said Jordan.

"Well?" said Beverly.

Jordan searched for words to describe the day, picturing it all in his head.

"It could have been worse."

Beverly smiled and raised her glass, clinking it with Jordan's.

"I'll toast to that!"

When the meal was finished, they cleared the table, and then Beverly washed the dishes while Jordan dried them. They worked in silence until Jordan had put all the clean dishes away.

"So," he said, closing the cupboard and turning to his grandmother with a small smile, "is it showtime yet?"

"I don't know," Beverly said, laying her dish towel down on the counter. "I'm a bit tired, Jordy."

"Maybe just a quick one?"

Beverly winked. "Well, I guess I'm not too tired for that."

Years earlier Beverly had lived in New York City, where she and her friends had thrown enormous parties and worn outrageous outfits. To a lot of people, these gatherings might have seemed a little silly, but Beverly knew the power a costume had to transform the way a person thought about themself. Beverly's closet was full of memories of that time, stuffed to bursting with sequins, patterns and possibilities.

When he'd first come to live with her, Jordan had wanted to try on every single piece of clothing in her closet. He knew without a doubt that they were magical. And when he put them on, he felt powerful.

Tonight Beverly selected a bright green garment from a padded-silk hanger, and then Jordan carefully picked an outfit of his own.

"What about up top?" Beverly asked, gesturing to a row of mannequin heads that sat on a shelf too high for Jordan to reach. Resting on the heads were wigs in every color of the rainbow.

Jordan had done his hair just the way he liked it for his first day of school, and it was still smooth and silky to the touch.

"No," he said, "not tonight."

Back in his bedroom, Jordan got dressed. He brushed his long hair so it fell straight down, framing the sides of his face.

"Ready?" called Beverly.

Jordan looked in the mirror and nodded at himself. "Ready."

In the living room, Beverly had put an album on her old record player, and one of their favorite songs was curling its way out of the speakers. The music was jangly and upbeat, with just a hint of soulful sadness underneath.

Beverly was the first to start dancing. She wiggled her hips back and forth, and the sequined dress she wore—acid green and covered in giant eyeballs—waved to the rhythm of the beat.

Jordan joined in. The silvery robe he had on made him feel like Cleopatra, and he struck fierce, dramatic poses in time to the music.

They sang along to all their favorite parts and made up dance routines as

they went. When they reached the final song on the record, they were exhausted, but both Beverly and Jordan wore wide grins on their faces.

"I think we put on a pretty good show tonight," Beverly said, dabbing at her brow with a tissue before putting the record back into its sleeve.

Jordan paused. He suspected that if anyone at school saw how he and his grandmother spent their evenings, he'd have even fewer friends than Max did. But as he contemplated the silk of the robe as it draped across his arms, and the way it made him feel proud and confident, he knew there was nothing else that made him this happy.

"It was good," Jordan said. "But we definitely need more practice."

CHAPTER FOUR

The next day at school, Jordan practiced blending in. He kept quiet all through class, spent recess alone and ate lunch by himself. His invisibility act was working wonderfully, but he had to admit that he felt a little lonely. Still, it was better than being picked on.

That afternoon Ms. Davenport made an announcement.

"Yesterday we talked about ourselves as individuals," she said, clasping her hands and hugging them tightly to her chest, "but moving forward from today, we will be working together. One of the greatest things about sharing with another person is being able to bring out the best in each other."

Around the room there were confused murmurs. A few kids seemed intrigued, but most of the students, like Jordan, looked concerned.

"There's no need to be nervous," said Ms. Davenport. "You're going to be picking a partner and working in pairs to create a presentation. It can be about anything you like—as long as it tells us something new about you both. At the end of the week, each pair will have the chance to present to the class."

Some of the students smiled and high-fived, but Jordan didn't join in.

Giving a presentation in his first week of school was not in his plan. And he didn't want anyone to bring out the best part of himself—especially not in front of the whole class.

"Remember to listen to one another," said Ms. Davenport. "Be honest and be open. And above all, be creative!"

There was a total scramble as the teacher finished speaking, and soon the whole room had paired up, leaving Jordan all by himself. There was only one other student left without a partner.

Max.

The two made eye contact across the room, and Jordan offered a tiny smile that Max did not return. Clearing his throat, Jordan felt the worry party in his stomach rage.

As the rest of their classmates spread out to different areas of the room, Max sat firmly at his desk, which was covered in pages torn from his notebook and pens in three different colors.

"You come over here," he said, crossing his arms. "It's where all my stuff is."

Jordan nodded and crossed the room to sit next to his partner, hoping they could come up with something

simple for their presentation and that this would all be over soon.

Max, as it turned out, didn't share Jordan's hope.

"You're in luck," he said, puffing out his chest and sweeping a pile of paper off his desk and onto the floor. "I have so many ideas. I think we should make a movie—feature-length! I can direct the whole thing, and it will be brilliant."

Ms. Davenport, walking by, noticed the mess on the carpet.

"I certainly hope you're planning to clean this up before you get started," she said.

"Sheesh!" said Max, stooping to pick up his papers. "These people have no appreciation for the artistic temperament. So what do you think of my idea?"

"Hmm," said Jordan.

"Hmm?" said Max.

A full-length feature film sounded like a good way to get a lot of people to notice you, which was exactly what Jordan didn't want at Massey Elementary.

"You seem interesting," Max said, nodding as he looked Jordan up and down. "I bet you'd be a great actor."

"I don't know about that," said Jordan.

Max slumped in his seat. "If you don't like it," he said, "then what's your big idea?"

Jordan considered this. He was about to open his mouth when the bell rang out, a high, twanging tone like when his grandmother tuned her acoustic guitar. It was the end of the day.

"Just like an actor," Max said. "Lost in your own world. You better come over to my house. We've got some serious work to do."

CHAPTER FIVE

It was a short walk to Max's place from the school, and soon they arrived at a small house with a yellow door and a porch cluttered with plants and bicycles.

Jordan called Beverly to tell her that he would be coming home late, and he heard his grandmother's voice rise three octaves when she said, "You're going over to a friend's place?"

"Well," said Jordan, "not exactly."

Max ran up the steps and fished around in his pockets for a key. When he finally found it, he opened the door so swiftly that Jordan swore the doorknob would bust a hole right through the wall.

"I'm home!" yelled Max.

As Jordan passed through the doorway, he suddenly understood why the volume on his classmate's voice seemed to be turned up so high. Max's house was *LOUD*. The sound of power tools shrieked from down below while a wailing guitar that was nothing like his grandmother's came from up the stairs.

Max kicked his off sneakers without untying them and pointed a thumb in the direction of the music. "My sister Tracy." He flipped his thumb to point downstairs. "My sister Connie."

"Huh?" said Jordan.

Max sighed deeply, as if explaining any further was exhausting and unnecessary. "Connie's an industrial sculptor," he said, "and Tracy plays in a metal band."

"Oh," said Jordan.

"Our parents won't be home for hours, so it's going to be pretty noisy till then. Come on. We can work at the kitchen table."

Jordan's eyes bounced around, taking in all the details of the room. Old diner signs hung on the walls next to paintings that looked like they'd been done by a sugared-up kindergartner. All around them were abstract sculptures made of pieces of rusted metal. By contrast, Jordan and Beverly's apartment was quite plain. Of course, the average visitor had no idea just how many treasures

were hidden inside Beverly's closet. That was how Jordan liked it.

But he had to admit, this was a very interesting house.

"So," said Max, "have you come to your senses yet?"

"Huh?"

"About the movie! We have to make one. *Come on.*"

Jordan had done a lot of thinking as they'd walked here from school, but the whiny drilling from downstairs and the throaty growling from upstairs had his head all in a spin, and he found that here, in Max's house, he couldn't think straight.

It wasn't as if he'd come up with any ideas of his own. At least, not yet.

"Fine," said Jordan. "We'll make a movie."

"Yes!!" shouted Max, pumping his fist in the air. "This is going to be incredible!"

Jordan wasn't so sure.

CHAPTER SIX

First, they needed a camera.

"We'll borrow my sister's phone," said Max.

"Which one?" asked Jordan, wondering which of the two sisters would be more likely to lend Max their phone for the time it would take to film a feature-length movie.

"We'll try Connie first," said Max. "Tracy's still mad at me for saying her band's latest song sounds like nu metal."

Jordan nodded, even though he had no clue what Max was talking about. He wasn't even sure what it would be like to have a sibling who was mad at you, but it sounded kind of...nice.

Together Jordan and Max trooped downstairs.

The basement smelled like a cross between a cave and a laundry room. It was good in a weird way, and Jordan found that once he started, he couldn't stop sniffing the dank air.

Every available surface was over-flowing with rusty old machine parts and scary-looking tools. In one corner a tall teenage girl with bright blue hair wielded a welding torch pointed at pieces of pipe.

"Brother walking!" Max called, weaving his way through the clutter on the floor like it was a well-worn path.

"Flame off!" Connie called back, extinguishing the fiery blue tip of her torch. It matched her hair perfectly.

Connie lifted the heavy face mask she'd been wearing and gave Max a look.

"This is Jordan," Max said. "We're partners. At school. We've got to make a movie for this big class project. Can we borrow your phone?"

"I don't see that happening," said Connie. "You have no respect for my things."

Max bristled. "Is this about your last piece?"

"The one that you used as a bowl for your cereal."

"There weren't any clean dishes!"

"And whose job was it to wash them?"

For the first time since Jordan had met him, Max fell silent.

"Come on," Max said, when they'd made it to the top of the stairs, "Tracy's usually nicer. Kind of."

Upstairs, the door to Tracy's room was practically pulsating from the heavy bass of the music inside.

"Brother entering!" Max called, knocking on the door. He had to pound three times before his sister emerged.

Tracy's room had the look of a tidy but haunted old manor, with ornately carved wooden furniture and framed posters of bands with long, hard-to-pronounce names. Tracy herself was dressed all in black, with her hair in long braids. She had hung up her guitar on the wall and was blaring a song from her stereo that sounded like a garbage truck running over a mile-long pothole.

"Can we borrow your phone?" Max asked. "It's important."

"What is so important?" Tracy asked, ignoring Jordan altogether.

"A project. For school."

"And Connie said no?"

"Uh-huh. Please? We'll be careful, I swear!"

"Fine," Tracy said, standing up from her desk and revealing her shoes— six-inch platform boots that made her tower over Jordan and Max. She picked up her phone from her bedside table.

Max made a grab for it, but she shook her head and held it out of reach.

"*Tomorrow*."

he wondered how he was going to work up the nerve to act in front of a camera. It was easy to have that kind of confidence here at home, but outside was a whole other story.

He didn't have long to worry though. The next day at school, Max raced up to Jordan on the schoolyard, clutching Tracy's phone to his chest like it was a wounded bird.

"Tracy says she's going on a day-long digital detox!" Max said. "We have exactly twenty-four hours to make our movie!"

During class, Ms. Davenport gave them free time to work on their projects. Max handed Jordan the script he'd stayed up late working on.

"You're sure we'll have time to film all of this?" Jordan asked, flipping through the fat stack of pages.

"I guess so," said Jordan. "He's kind of...strange."

"Sounds like my kind of people," said Beverly, taking a sip of her drink.

"Maybe," said Jordan. "But he's loud. And he's not always very nice. He's sort of pushy."

Beverly smiled. "Definitely my kind of people."

Showtime that night was shorter than usual. As Jordan took off his grandmother's powder-pink beehive wig,

"Of course!" said Max. "You have to trust my vision! My optometrist says it's perfect."

Jordan wasn't sure this was exactly what Max's doctor was referring to, but he didn't want to argue, so he studied the script to learn his lines.

Meanwhile Max was already at the window, looking out as he held up his fingers like a frame.

"We'll start filming at lunch!"

Lunchtime came all too soon for Jordan's liking. He'd barely finished the soup in his thermos when Max started tugging him by the sleeve toward the schoolyard.

"This first scene's of just me," he said, taking out his sister's phone and passing the precious device over to Jordan, "so you'll have to film."

Jordan often used Beverly's phone to play games, watch videos or do searches online, but he'd never filmed anything himself.

"Hold it sideways," said Max. "It's better that way. And make sure my lighting is good."

"Don't you need a costume?" asked Jordan.

"Way ahead of you."

Max unzipped his jacket and unbuttoned his shirt to reveal a T-shirt that said *OUR HERO*. He had a small red cape tied around his neck.

"Okay," said Jordan, tapping the screen to make the phone record.

Max launched into a monologue that he'd memorized from his script, then took off running across the schoolyard.

Jordan liked running—he and Beverly sometimes went for jogs together on Sunday mornings. It helped Jordan to relax and clear his head, putting one foot in front of the other, feeling the strength of his legs beneath him.

But this was not jogging with his grandmother. Sprinting after Max, keeping the camera pointed squarely at his partner, was something different altogether. It made Jordan's legs and lungs burn. Max seemed to have a bottomless well of energy, shouting and pointing all the way, but Jordan had trouble keeping up. The camera's frame wobbled as he ran.

Finally Max climbed to the top of the jungle gym and delivered his last line. "Now, who will challenge me, the hero of heroes? The righter of wrongs?

The towering turret of…uh, darn." He broke character and turned to face the camera. "Just cut, okay? Cut. We'll try it again."

"Again?" said Jordan, trying to catch his breath.

"Fine," said Max. "We can take a break. Let me look at what you shot."

Jordan handed over the phone, and Max played back the scene. Max's face darkened like a storm cloud as he watched. Finally he spoke.

"This is what you got? This is terrible! You couldn't even keep the camera straight!"

"Maybe if you hadn't been running so fast."

"But this movie needs action! Adventure! It has to capture the real me!"

The real Max, Jordan thought, wasn't anything like this superhero character he had created. The real Max wasn't doing good and righting wrongs.

The real Max was kind of mean.

"Fine," said Max. "We can fix this later. Let's just shoot the next scene."

CHAPTER EIGHT

The next scene, Max explained, would require some very special effects.

He led Jordan deep into the back field, where there was a cluster of gnarled trees that had already shed their leaves. Max picked up a handful and crushed them into a flaky powder in his fist.

"This," he said, "is perfect."

Jordan looked longingly toward the school. "Aren't we going to be late getting back to class?"

"Not to worry," said Max. "I explained it all to Ms. Davenport, and she told me to take all the time I need with my movie."

"*Us*, you mean," said Jordan. "With *our* movie."

"Yeah, sure. Now let's get to work!"

After spending the better part of an hour crumbling up all the leaves they could find, Max lifted the bottom of his shirt and held it out like a hammock. He scooped the leafy powder into the hollow of his shirt and then rolled it up to protect their hard work from any pesky wind.

Using only one hand, he scaled the nearest tree and staked out a spot on one of its branches.

"Okay," said Max once he was in position. "On the count of three

I'm going to jump down, spraying leaf confetti everywhere. Got it?"

"But why?" Jordan asked, craning his neck.

"Didn't you read my script? This is the scene where Our Hero unleashes a plague of bloodsucking mutant insects! It's going to be epic!"

"I thought he was supposed to be a good guy?" Jordan said, wishing he'd read the script more carefully.

"He's complicated! No one understands him, so he has to punish them!"

"What, the whole world?" Jordan was not particularly impressed with his partner's logic.

"Come on!" said Max. "The day's almost over! We've got to do this now!"

Jordan shook his head but said okay. He aimed the camera and counted down from three while Max readied himself for his jump.

"Three…"

Max raised his shoulders up to his ears.

"Two…"

Jordan paused. "Are you sure this is—"

"One!" shouted Max. He flung himself off the branch, shooting out a cloud of dead-leaf powder as he flew through the air with an impressive high kick.

Jordan had to admit, Max really did look awesome.

But as soon as Max landed—miraculously unhurt—Jordan knew something was wrong.

"Did you see that?" asked Max. "I was incredible! Let me see, let me see, let me see!"

He took the phone from Jordan, and then the wide grin he'd been wearing turned itself upside down.

"You took a picture!" he said. "A blurry picture! You can't even see me through the leaves! Some cinematographer you are!"

Jordan was embarrassed at his mistake, but more than that, he was mad.

"If I'm so bad with the camera," he said, "then you can film the whole thing yourself. I quit!"

If there had been a door to slam, he would have slammed it. Instead Jordan turned and walked away.

"Wait!" said Max. "Come back! Please!"

But Jordan was already gone.

CHAPTER NINE

"I never knew you to be a quitter," Beverly said to Jordan that night as they finished doing the dishes.

Jordan sighed. "I'm not. But this kid, Max, he's just impossible."

"Hmm," said Beverly.

"I'm going to tell Ms. Davenport tomorrow that we can't work together," said Jordan. "It's just too hard. Max never listens—it's all about what he wants."

"Hmm," said Beverly, as she washed the last spoon.

"Now," said Jordan, "is it showtime yet? Please?"

"Just wait," said his grandmother. "Have you tried telling this Max what you'd like to do? Have you ever mentioned, for instance, that you don't agree with his ideas?"

"Hmm," said Jordan.

"Hmm?" said Beverly.

"Well, no. Not exactly."

Jordan didn't want to talk about it anymore.

So Beverly dropped the subject, and soon they were moving and grooving in the living room to the tunes of one of Jordan's very favorite singers. Her voice was brassy and tight, like someone you wouldn't want to mess with. Just hearing her words made Jordan feel stronger. He was proud of himself for standing up to Max the way he did, but it hadn't been easy.

Then there was a knock on the door.

"I'll get it," said Beverly, lifting the arm of the record player to bring the music to a halt.

Moments later she returned to where Jordan was not exactly hiding behind the sofa.

"You have a visitor," she said.

"Me?"

"I believe he said his name is Max."

"Hmm."

"Now Jordy," said Beverly, squeezing his knee, "you think about this. Nobody's perfect. And this Max seems like he's very sorry."

"He should be."

Beverly smiled. "Maybe you should tell him that yourself."

Jordan considered it. He had on a turquoise blouse of Beverly's that came almost to his knees, with a big gold belt around his middle, and a bright white wig that stuck out at odd angles and reminded his grandmother of one of her very favorite artists. His name was Andy, and he made paintings of soup cans and celebrities.

Before Max had so rudely interrupted, Jordan had been dancing to a song that made him feel like he was someone really special. And if he held his eyes shut just so, he still felt that way now.

Jordan knew it wouldn't be easy to face Max. To explain to him that Max had been wrong to be so pushy, that just because a person was quiet didn't mean they didn't have ideas to share.

These clothes Jordan had on, and this wig—they were powerful. But even more than that, they were what made Jordan feel like the very best version of himself.

Taking a deep breath, he held himself up as tall as he could. Then he went to talk to Max.

CHAPTER TEN

The person standing in the doorway didn't look anything like Jordan's partner from class. Where Max carried himself with an air of smugness and irritation, this person looked embarrassed and regretful. This person looked small.

Still feeling his power, Jordan crossed his arms in front of his chest.

"Hello."

"Hey," said Max, not looking up, as if he was speaking to his shoes.

Jordan raised his head higher, feeling the weight of the wig and the confidence it gave him. This ability to transform himself was his superpower.

"What do you want?"

"I," said Max, "I...I...I'm sorry."

He articulated the word *sorry* like it was the first time he'd ever spoken it out loud and he wasn't quite sure that he was pronouncing it right.

"Sorry?" said Jordan. "For what, exactly?"

Max's eyes never left the ground. "I'm sorry for yelling at you. And for being such a crummy partner. It wasn't right. I'm really sorry."

Jordan nodded, and then, realizing Max still hadn't looked him in the face, he spoke.

"No," said Jordan. "It wasn't right. Thank you for saying so."

There was a pause, and then a car horn blared outside. Looking out the door, Jordan saw two familiar faces leaning out the passenger-side window of a parked car.

"Has he apologized yet?" shouted Tracy.

"Yeah," added Connie, "and did he mention how he cried when he got home?"

Max raised his head to call back to his sisters. "Just give me a couple of minutes, okay? Sheesh!"

As Max turned back to face him, Jordan noticed that his partner's eyes were puffy—he *had* been crying! Crying over Jordan quitting the movie.

And now Max was looking at Jordan, really taking him in—his outfit, his wig, his *everything*.

Max's sorry frown changed then, his face breaking into a huge grin.

"Come in a minute," said Jordan. "I've got something to show you."

In the living room, Max couldn't hide his excitement.

"This is amazing!" he said. "You do this every night?"

"Only when it's showtime," said Jordan, taking off his wig to scratch his head.

"Most weeknights," said Beverly with a wink. "And sometimes a Saturday matinee."

"It's perfect!" said Max. "*This* is what we should do! A live show—something spectacular! I mean…if you want to, that is."

Jordan looked at Beverly, but her expression—underneath her fluorescent-yellow beehive—was totally blank.

"Up to you, kiddo. We've got more than enough costumes to share."

Jordan thought about it. A superhero doesn't hide their power when called upon, and a superhero isn't embarrassed about being special either. Showing Max what he could do, and who he really was, felt wonderful. Maybe with his new friend by his side, Jordan could be brave enough to show the rest of his classmates too.

"Yes," he said, nodding. "Absolutely."

CHAPTER ELEVEN

His first week of school had gone by so quickly, Jordan could hardly believe it when Friday morning arrived. He could feel electricity shooting through his body as he packed his bag for school—one of Beverly's extra-large totes, absolutely stuffed with costumes and wigs for his presentation with Max.

The whole show played itself over and over again in his head, and everything went just the way it had in their rehearsals.

But there was no more time to practice. Today was the day.

Each of the pairs of partners in Ms. Davenport's class would take turns presenting, and Jordan and Max had been chosen to go last.

Although Max had tried to push Jordan into being the one to explain to their teacher that they were no longer making a movie, in the end he had done it himself. Ms. Davenport hadn't seemed too pleased that they had used so much class time on the film only to ditch it altogether, but she said she would be glad to see whatever they had prepared.

All day long, Jordan squirmed in his chair. He imagined all his classmates jumping to their feet when he and Max took their bows. Maybe this secret superhero identity, which he'd kept to himself for such a long time, was going to open up a whole new world of friends.

He'd liked having Max as a friend for the last few days. It made him feel lighter to share jokes and stories with someone else from school. He had felt a little less alone and a little less like an alien at Massey Elementary.

That afternoon, as they watched their fellow students, two at a time, get up and present, Jordan noticed Max's foot twitching, faster and faster—*thump-thump-thumping* against the linoleum floor like he was tapping out a rapid-fire Morse code message.

"Hey," Jordan whispered, "are you okay?"

Max blew out a giant breath. "Fine," he said. "I'm totally fine."

Jordan could tell that wasn't true.

"We'll be great," he said. "You'll see!"

But Max seemed less than convinced.

Finally it was their turn. Jordan and Max had watched their classmates talk all day about the things they liked—rare rodents and Korean boy bands, robots and famous hockey players. Sure, some of the pairs had used props or played games with the class, but no one else had prepared a true performance the way they had.

Changing into their costumes in the washroom just before they were up, Max turned to Jordan. His eyes were wide and pleading.

"Are we sure we want to do this?" he whispered.

Jordan gave his long black wig one final adjustment in the mirror and then nodded.

"Of course," Jordan said. "It's showtime."

Their performance wasn't exactly the same as Jordan and Beverly's shows at home, and it didn't exactly go the way they had rehearsed it either.

Max, as it turned out, wasn't quite as much of a triple threat as he'd advertised, but they'd worked hard to get him up to speed. He'd had lots of ideas about choreography and had managed to incorporate a scene from his movie script too. Unfortunately, Max's nerves undid some of their hard work, and he was several beats behind and flubbed his lines three times.

Max even tripped on the train of his dress, and Jordan had to cover for him while his partner sorted out his wardrobe. But when the time came for their closing number, they really sold it. They didn't just mouth the words the way Jordan and Beverly did at home— they sang and danced, their moves completely in sync. When the final chorus came raining down, Jordan was sure they would be met with thunderous applause.

Only they weren't. Just as they finished, the bell rang out its high, twanging tone, and without so much as a half-hearted clap or a backward glance, their classmates got up from their seats and hurried out the door.

Jordan and Max turned to look at each other. After all of their hard work, that was it?

Behind her desk, Ms. Davenport offered a smile that didn't quite reach her eyes.

"Thank you both for sharing," she said. "That was certainly a unique performance. Maybe next time your presentation can be a bit more…focused."

Jordan took off his wig and felt his superpower slowly drain away.

He barely heard it when one of his straggling classmates, who had given a speech with their partner about classic comic books, piped up from the back of the room, "I like your lipstick."

CHAPTER TWELVE

Jordan didn't feel much like celebrating. While he and Max had planned to have a pizza party for two after school to toast their big success, Jordan wished now that he could go home and be alone.

As they waited on the curb for Beverly to pick them up, Jordan didn't even want to look at the bag of costumes at his feet. What a disappointment the whole thing had been.

He'd imagined his classmates smiling and cheering them on, but instead they hadn't really reacted at all. That was almost worse than if they had booed or laughed—it was like Jordan and Max were too strange to even acknowledge.

But Max didn't seem bothered. He hummed to himself as they waited and tapped his fingers on his thighs like he was playing the world's tiniest drum solo.

"I still think we were great," Max said. "I was so nervous getting up there. But it really was fun performing, wasn't it? And you were fantastic!"

Jordan smiled a tiny smile with just one side of his mouth.

"Thanks," he said. "No one else seemed to think so."

What would it mean, now that his secret identity was out? Would he have new critics to face on the schoolyard? Every superhero had their supervillain, after all.

"So?" said Max, interrupting Jordan's thoughts. "Who cares? Nobody at school's ever liked me anyway. At least now we've got each other. And our act!"

As Jordan gazed down the street, trying to spot his grandmother's car in the snarl of traffic, he thought about Max's words.

It *had* felt good putting on his costume and letting other people see it. Like he had used his superpower for good. Even better, he'd found someone new to share that magic with.

It made Jordan feel stronger just thinking about it.

Max understood. He wasn't a perfect friend or partner, but he knew what was important. And if any dastardly villains showed up, Jordan knew he wouldn't face them alone.

Deep in Jordan's stomach, he felt the wobble of his worries as their wild party ended and they finally packed up and went home.

They would be back, he knew. But not today.

"Seriously," Max said, "who cares what people think?"

Jordan turned to face his friend and smiled.

"Not me."

Genie Meanie

Mahtab Narsimhan

illustrated by
Michelle Simpson

Kiara can't believe her luck—a genie of her very own to fix all her problems! But what is she supposed to do when the genie decides he is on vacation and won't listen to her?

I stared. And stared. A minute passed, then two. Zayn walked around the room, examining everything, smirking at me now and then.

"You're a real, live *genie*?" I asked.

"Yes and yes."

"The magical kind?" I said.

"Bingo!"

"One that can grant *three* wishes?" I said, fingers crossed behind my back.

"Oui, madame!" he said. "And make that unlimited wishes. *Three* is so last millennium."

"As many as I like?" I asked, just so there was no confusion. I was already making a mental list of all the things I wanted.

"Si, señorita!" he said.

"Someone who will do my every bidding!" I said. "Like in the Aladdin story?"

"Whoa!" said Zayn, tossing his stinky turban onto my bed. "We'll have to discuss that. But before we do anything, I need a shower and something to eat."

I stared at him. "My name is Kiara, and you've forgotten the magic word."

He raised an eyebrow. "We don't use magic words these days. Too old-fashioned."

"I meant *please*," I said. "And *thank you*. *Sorry* too, if you've done something wrong."

Zayn stopped in mid eye roll when I glared at him. "*Please* get me something to eat or you'll be very *sorry*," he said with a charming smile. "*Thank you*."

He did smell like an overcooked curry and badly needed a shower.

"I'll get you a snack. The bathroom is right there."

Gran had never told me *anything* about a genie. How did she get him? Was Zayn real or had the stress of facing Matt tomorrow made me lose my mind already? I stared at the empty bottle. The label explained his name, *Zayn* Garam Masala. I'd make him explain everything else to me later.

Mom was cleaning up in the kitchen.

"May I have a snack before bed?" I asked.

She looked surprised but agreed. "Would you like an apple with peanut butter?"

"How about some more of your delicious curry and rice *plus* the apple with peanut butter?"

"I thought you'd eaten your fill at dinner, but all right," said Mom with a laugh. "Once you finish, bring the dirty dishes down and put them in the dishwasher, please."

I carried the food upstairs on a tray, shut my door and piled some books and stuffies against it. Early warning system in case Mom decided to drop in while I was negotiating my wish list with Zayn.

Minutes later he walked out of the bathroom, wearing a pair of shorts and my favorite yellow T-shirt and smelling of my watermelon shampoo. A whiff of garam masala still clung to him. It would probably take another thousand years of scrubbing to get rid of *that* smell.

"Hey!" I said. "Who said you could wear my clothes?"

"My clothes stank. And these are so soft and comfortable," he said.

"Eat, and then we talk," I said, pushing the tray toward him. "I'll give you my wish list. The first thing I want is for you to take care of the bully, Matt."

Zayn sat cross-legged on the carpet and inhaled the food, pausing only to say, "Your mother is a great cook!" Within seconds the plates were wiped clean. He burped loudly.

"Manners!" I said.

Zayn burped even louder. "You may ask your questions now, Kiara."

"How did you get into that bottle?"

Zayn shook his head. "Long story, and I'm too tired to tell you now. Next?"

"Can everyone see you, or am I the only one?"

Before he could answer, there was a knock on my door. I jumped up so quickly I almost fell over. How would I explain why I had another kid in my room without permission? Mom was going to have a cow.

SUZANNE SUTHERLAND is an author and editor of books for young people, and she is passionate about inclusive and engaging storytelling. Her debut novel, *When We Were Good,* was selected for ALA's Rainbow Book List, and *Under the Dusty Moon* was a Toronto Public Library Top Ten Recommended Read for Teens. Suzanne lives in Toronto.